The Why Are You Here Cafe

Copyright © 2022 Bradford Holmwood All rights reserved

The characters and events portrayed in this book are fictitious. Any similarity to real persons, living or dead, is coincidental and not intended by the author.

No part of this book may be reproduced, or stored in a retrieval system, or transmitted in any form or by any means, electronic, mechanical, photocopying, recording, or otherwise, without express written permission of the publisher.

Cover design by: Richard Drumming
ISBN: 9798815523784
Printed in the United States of America

-1-

Sometimes, when you least expect it, and probably when you need it most, you'll suddenly be in a whole new environment, meet new people, and see all kinds of new things. I've had the experience of walking down a dark, lonely road one night. Now that I think about it, the scene is exactly the portrayal of my life at that stage. I'm lost, and I'm lost on the journey of life. I don't know where the road under my feet leads, or why I'm going in that direction.

I left my job and took a week off trying to escape anything work related. Actually, my job isn't that bad. Although it can be frustrating. But more critical than most. I sit in a cubicle every day and work for ten to twelve hours. Later, when I get promoted, at most I move into an independent office, and my working hours become twelve to fourteen hours. I endure it. I can't stop thinking. Should life be like this? Are there any other options out there?

When I was in high school, I worked hard to get into a good college. After I finished college, I worked hard to find a job. After that, I came to work for a company and spent all of my time trying to get promoted. Now, I questioned those who have traveled this path before me, and I suspect they are simply repeating the guidance they were given.

Their advice is good, but it doesn't help you truly succeed. I feel like I've been so busy trading my life for money that the deal doesn't seem like a good deal. It was in this confused state of mind that I discovered the "why are you here cafe".

Whenever I tell people this story, they say it's "mysterious," or something from the Twilight Zone, or Black Mirror. "Twilight Zone" was an old TV series. The environment in which the characters are at first glance very ordinary, but the ending of the story is mysterious. From time to time, I have moments of hesitation, suspecting that my experience was not real. Whenever this happens, I go to my desk at home, open the drawer, look at the text on the menu Kayleen gave me, and remind myself that it all happened.

I never re-traced that road and never went back to that cafe. There's a little voice inside me that even if I could go back to that location, the cafe wouldn't be there. The only reason I found it at that moment, that night, is that I needed that cafe. The pavilion only exists because of that.

Maybe one day, I'll go back and look for it. Maybe one night, I'll stand once again in front of its door. Then go in

and tell Kayleen, Jacob, and Beth… Well, if she's there…
And tell them how that night changed my life. How the
questions they threw at me made me think in a whole new
light and discovery.

Who knows, maybe then I will chat all night with other
people who got lost and strayed into the "why are you here
in the cafe".

Maybe someday I will write a book to tell everyone about
that experience, and we can consider it a contribution to let
more people know the meaning of such a cafe.

The interstate was backed up as I sat in the stop and go traffic. If anyone walked by, it would look like they were sprinting compared to us as we sat in our cars stopping and going, but mostly stopping. After an hour, the slow-moving traffic came to a complete standstill. I pressed the radio's search button and searched for signs of intelligent life, but found nothing.

Twenty minutes passed without anyone's car moving forward. So people got out of their cars to stretch their legs and talk to others about why they thought the traffic had stopped. While this doesn't help traffic jams, it is nice to also complain about it with other people.

Ahead of me, a van owner kept saying that if he didn't get to the hotel by six, they would cancel his reservation. On my left, a woman in a convertible was on the phone, complaining about the inefficiency of the highway system. Behind me, a carload of youth baseball players almost drove their teacher crazy. I could hear her voice as she shouted. She never wanted to volunteer for any events again. This section of the road seemed to be a long snake full of resentment, and I was just a small scale on it.

Twenty minutes later, there was still no sign of the traffic moving. Finally, a police car drove over from the lawn divider in the middle of the road. The police car stopped every 100 feet, presumably to explain the situation ahead. I thought to myself, 'I hope the police have riot gear, otherwise I fear for their safety!'

Everyone waited anxiously, hoping that the police car would come soon so they could find out what had happened. Finally, the police came to our section of the road. A female police officer told everyone that about five miles ahead, a fuel tanker suspected of carrying toxic substances overturned and blocked the entire road. She said we have two options: one is to turn around and find another way - there is really no "other way" to be found; the other is to stay put and wait for the obstacles ahead to be cleared. She said it would take maybe another hour.

I watched the police car drive down to the next group of disgruntled drivers. The driver of the van said again that he was worried that he could not get to the hotel at six o'clock, and my patience finally ran out.

"I always run into this kind of trouble when I go out to relax," I muttered.

Just like the children I met when I was a child because I lived close by, the driver nearby has also become my new friend. I told them I couldn't wait any longer and tried another route. The van driver was still telling people about the cancellation of the room, and after the last sentence, he got in his van and moved a little out of my way so I could maneuver my car around. I crossed the barrier and drove off in a new direction.

Before hitting the road, I had printed out the driving directions I found online, which I thought was a smart move. "There's no need for a map," I thought, "just follow these simple and clear instructions." But now they were useless. So I took out my phone and prepared to open the map. "GPS not found", was on the screen. I used to always carry an atlas with me when I was driving. I wish I still did.

"Even if I find the highway exit, it's useless. Anyway, I don't know how to get there at all." I muttered to myself aloud, and my mental state became worse and worse.

After 28 miles, I finally saw an exit.

"Damn it," I thought as I pulled up to the exit ramp. "There are no gas stations or fast-food restaurants at this highway stop. This is probably the only off ramp in the world that has nothing, and I just went down it." I looked to the left. It was empty, and then to the right, it was also empty.

"Okay," I said, "it seems to be the same no matter which way I go."

I drove to the right and made a mental note of going west, reminding myself to turn right at the next intersection. That way, I can always get back on my way north. This section of the road is a two-way and two-lane, one leading off into the distance, the other leading to the direction of the coming. I have absolutely no idea which one to choose. There are very few passing vehicles here, and fewer houses on the roadside. Occasionally I glimpsed a solitary house, a few family farms, and beyond that there were only forest and meadows.

After an hour, I was hopelessly lost. I only passed a narrow intersection where several signs stood to make it easy to see that something was wrong. After driving for 40 miles, not only did I not see a single person, but I also drove down a road with the word "No" in its name, similar to the road name "Ancient Road No. 65", and the surrounding area was desolate.

Then came another intersection, almost as small as the one I had passed before. In desperation, I turned right here, thinking; I don't know where I am, but at least I'm in the right direction. But the name of the next road also has the word "No" in it, which was really unfortunate.

It was nearly 8pm; the sun was setting, and the day was about to pass, and I was getting more and more frustrated. I absently wondered if the van driver had gotten to his hotel on time or if they had canceled his reservation.

"If I had known this, I should have stayed on the highway and waited," I retorted. "I originally planned to leave without delaying an hour, but now I have not only wasted two hours, and now I'm lost."

Although the current situation is not to blame my car, hitting it fixed nothing, but I punched the roof, anyway.

10 miles, 15 miles, 20 miles later, the front is still empty. I

only have half a tank of gas left. Now, I definitely can't drive back, and the remaining gas definitely can not hold out in the traffic jam; even if I can, I may not find the way I came from. Even if I make it back, there are still no gas stations from here to there.

My only option was to bite the bullet and drive, hoping there was a gas station and a place to eat ahead. My frustration level is the opposite of the pointer on the fuel gauge, and it is rising higher and higher.

Because there are a lot of troubles at work and life at home, I traveled far, in search of a place to relax; things at home are already annoying enough, I really didn't expect it to be so annoying when I went out. The purpose of the trip is obviously to relax and get motivated again.

"What a strange word," I thought, "Go hard, and you're going to lose a thousand miles. You're going to be pumped up, but you're still going to lose a thousand miles."

The clouds were a little pink and orange, reflecting the afterglow of the sky, but my attention was on the road, full of worry about the worsening situation, and I paid little attention to the sky. There were still no other cars on the road.

I looked again at the end of the road to see if there was any shadow of a gas station. "Less than a quarter tank of gas left and the gauge is still going even further down," I said aloud.

The last time I slept in the car was on my way home from college. That was years ago, and I didn't intend to let history repeat itself. But unfortunately, the situation in front of me was more and more like that time.

"I need to get some sleep," I thought. "In case the car runs out of gas, I need to be strong enough to walk somewhere to get help."

I saw a light just as the oil gauge needle was about to slide below the red line marked with the letter E. Considering my current situation; I drove back a few miles and turned left at the previous intersection. In fact, there was no sign of anyone on the road on the left, but I still turned left. At least this road doesn't start with the word "old". I just made my decision because of that.

"When a person goes to a desperate place, he will survive." I shouted. I got closer and closer to the light, and finally saw that it was a white street lamp, alone in the distance, emitting a bright light, even though there was nothing around it.

"Please, there must be someone here," I repeated like a mantra as I drove the last quarter of a mile between the streetlights. Sure enough, there was something under the light.

I got off the main road and pulled into a gravel parking lot. It surprised me to see a small rectangular white building with a pale blue neon sign on the roof with the name of the shop "Why Are You Here Cafe". Another surprise to me was that there were three other cars parked in the parking lot. "Where did they come from? Must be from the same place as me," I thought, since I hadn't seen another car on the road for at least an hour. "It's a good thing. Maybe they know how to get out of this ghost place and back to the interstate."

When I got out of the car, raised my arms above my head, cracked my aching back, rolled my shoulders, and walked towards the door of the cafe. In the dark sky hung a large crescent moon, and thousands of stars were shining. I opened the door of the cafe and the little bell on the doorknob rang, announcing my arrival. An appetizing aroma hit my nostrils, and it surprised me when I realized how hungry I was. I decided I would order three servings of whatever meal was emitting that aroma.

The cafe had a certain old restaurant charm. There was a circle of high stools with chrome bases and red cushions next to the long and narrow white bar. There is a row of red booths by the front window. Both had a table with a small glass jar for granulated sugar, a small silver jug containing, I guess, milk to add to the coffee, and accompanying salt and pepper shakers.

There is an old-fashioned cash register on the counter by the door, next to a wooden coat rack. This cafe was cozy, a place to sit and chat with friends for a long time. Too bad I didn't have a friend with me.
A server was talking to two people further in a box far away, but she turned her head and smiled and said to have a seat, sit down, anywhere."

Calming myself enough to give her a smile, I picked a booth by the door and slumped down onto the red plastic seat, only to notice that the chair was very new. It surprised me to see that everything in the cafe was new.

"The owner must think that the city will expand to this place eventually," I thought, "that's why he opened a new cafe in this place where there is no store in front of the village."

"Hi!" A greeting interrupted my real estate conversation.My thoughts on affordable prices and housing development opportunities. It was the server who had told me to sit before. She looked at me with a wide smile and

said, "My name is Kayleen. How are you?"
 "Hi Kayleen! My name is John, and I'm a little lost."
"So it seems, John," she replied with a playful smile.

The tone of her voice was so ambiguous that it was hard for me to tell if she was really saying my name was John or if she was confirming I was indeed lost.
"Why are you here, John?" she asked, cocking her head to the side.
"Hey, I encountered some unexpected situations on the road. I wanted to detour, but I got lost. I feel as if I am starving to death, and my gas tank almost bottomed out." After I complained, Kayleen smiled a naughty smile again.

"I promise you," she said, "we can definitely help you with the hunger problem. As for the rest, we'll see."

She took a menu from the front door shelf and handed it to me. I don't know if it's because of the lighting or mental exhaustion from driving too long, but I swear, the moment she handed me the menu, I saw the words on the menu blurred and then reappeared. "I must be too tired," I thought, putting the menu on the table.

Kayleen took a small order board out of her pocket. "Why don't you order something to drink first and then look at the menu carefully," she suggested. I ordered a glass of lemonade.

The experience of the day was totally unexpected. I spent hours driving down old, desolate roads, then I found a cafe in what seemed like the end of the world, and now I met a waitress with a mischievous smile. I picked up the menu and looked at the cover.

"Welcome to 'Why Are You Here Cafe'", the phrase occupies the top half of the entire cover. Below this line is a line of small black words: "Before ordering, please ask our service staff what the time you are here means."

"I hope it means that I can eat good food." I turned to the first page as I thought.

On the menu are the usual cafe meals. Breakfast is in the upper left column, sandwiches are in the lower left column, starters and salads are in the upper right column, and main courses are in the lower right column. I turned the menu over and was taken aback. I saw a big headline on the back of the menu, "Please think while waiting for your meal," and here are three questions:

Why are you here?

Are you afraid of death?

Are you satisfied?

"It's not the same feeling as casually watching sports news," I thought. Just as I was about to reread the three questions, Kayleen came back with the lemonade I asked for.

"Anything you want to eat?" she asked.

I flipped the menu back to the cover and pointed to the name of the cafe.

"What does it mean?"

"Well, everyone seems to have their own interpretation of the name," she replied. "Actually, most of us here simply refer to it as the 'Why Cafe'. Would you like to order now?"

I'm not ready. I thought I should put on my jacket and leave right away. This place is definitely unusual, and that unusual seems to me more spooky than unusual: "Sorry, Kayleen, I need some time to think about it."

"It's okay," she said. "Think slowly, and I'll ask you later. Besides, John," she said with a small smile, "don't worry, leave it to us."

I watched as Kayleen walked to the booth at the other end of the cafe, where a couple sat and the three of them started talking. No matter what topic they were talking about, everyone must be in a good mood, because all three were smiling.

"This place should be good," I thought. "Maybe I should order something to eat."

My attention returned to the menu. "There's no other choice," I thought. "My car is out of gas, and there doesn't seem to be any other place to eat within 200 miles. Although this place looks odd, nothing out of the ordinary has happened so far."

When I thought about this, my worries eased a little. Kayleen made a trip to the kitchen and came out walking past me with two strawberry rhubarb pies, which made me less worried. I especially love strawberry rhubarb pie, but the last time I had it was years ago. I guess that means I should be here for a while.

Strange questions aside, the menu items look delicious. Even though it wasn't breakfast time at all, I ordered one. Kayleen was still talking to the couple. I was already thinking about what to order, so I flipped the menu to the back again.

Why are you here?

It sounds odd for a restaurant to ask diners this question. Don't you know why someone came to your restaurant? When you come to a restaurant to eat alone, don't you know why you are here? I suspect I didn't understand the question.

Why are you here?

Kayleen came over and interrupted my thinking.

"Have you thought about what to order?"

I was about to answer, but remembered the line on the cover of the menu that guests can ask the server before ordering. "Almost figured it out," I said, pointing to the line. "What question can I ask you?"

"Oh, that." She smiled again.

I liked her smile more and more.

"Over the past few years, we've seen some changes in the guests who have been here," she said. "So we want to let everyone understand the 'why are you here' question. We first share with guests some things they might expect, so that they can better accept what they thought they could accept."

I was completely confused. Is she talking about a meal, a cafe, or something else entirely?

"If you're ready," she said, "I'll show the chef what you

ordered and let him give him some advice."

"Of course..." I felt even more confused. "Okay. Give me a copy. Breakfast. It's not breakfast time, but can you make it?"

"Would you like to order that?" she asked.

"Yes, that's right."

"No problem. Today's lunch time is long over, but tomorrow's breakfast time is closer."

I glanced at my watch. It was half past ten in the evening. "It's interesting how you look at things," I said.

Kayleen smiled. "Looking at things from a different perspective can sometimes help us solve problems."

She took my order and turned away. I watched her back towards the kitchen and saw that she had left the menu on the table.

Kayleen approached the order window, and I saw another man in the kitchen. He was holding the wooden spoon, apparently the man in charge of the kitchen. Kayleen leaned closer to the window and said a few words to him. He stuck his head out and glanced at me. Seeing that I was looking at him, he smiled and waved at me.

I waved to him too, which was a little funny. I don't have the habit of waving to chefs in cafes. Kayleen talked to the man for a few minutes, then put my order menu on the little round ticket holder, turned and walked towards me. The man straightened the ticket holder, looked at it for a while, and took it into the kitchen.

My attention returned to the menu. I reread the first question, "Why are you here?", and then Kayleen came to my booth and sat down across from me.

"That man was Jacob," she said. "He runs the cafe and cooks the food. He said he'd come out and see you later. I asked him if he had the meal you ordered. The problem, he said it was a lot, but he thought you could finish it."

"You still have this kind of special service."

She smiled. "Yes. Let's talk about this now." She pointed to the line on the cover of the menu that asked customers to ask the staff, "I see you've been reading the question on the back of the menu. This sentence is the same as that question."

I don't know how she knew I was looking at the question, but I didn't answer.

"That's it," she said. "It's one thing to look at a problem, it's another to change it."

"What do you mean?"

"This question sounds simple and seems completely irrelevant to most people. Influence," she replied, "but if you change the question a bit, you can change some things."

I looked at her in confusion and said, "Change some things? What? It means I can't eat here, or do I run out of things I ordered and have to get something else?"

"No," the look on her face suddenly turned serious, "it's a much bigger change than that."

I really didn't understand what she was going to say, but she was clearly not joking. "I don't understand."

Kayleen pointed to the menu: "We do not ask this question of others, but you ask it of yourself and you will no longer be who you used to be."

It startled me. Not the me I used to be? What does that mean? I suddenly felt like I was standing on the edge of a steep cliff. I don't know if the next step she takes me forward will cause immediate death, or eternal happiness?

"It's pretty much what you think," she said with a smile, "but it's not as exaggerated."

Before I could ask her how she knew what I was thinking, she continued, "Don't worry about it. I'll explain it to you. You read the first question on the menu, but read it with an aloof attitude, like a street sign you glance at."

I glanced down at the menu quickly. To my surprise, the question above is no longer "Why are you here?".

It was now "Why am *I* here?".

Immediately after I finished reading it, the line changed back to "Why are you here?".

"What's going on?" I asked excitedly. "Did the menu change? Did **you** do it?"

"John, I don't think you're ready for the answer to this question."

"What do you mean by that? How the hell did you do that? How did the words on the menu change?" I was completely confused, not sure what was going on, or if I was going to stay here trying to figure it out. Then Kayleen caught my attention again with a question.

"John, did you see the text after the menu changed?"

"Of course I did. When I first read it, it was another line, and then it changed to the current line. Why is that?"

Kayleen turned the menu to the front and pointed to the phrase "before ordering...". "Yes, John," she explained.

"The question you saw, the question that became different..."

"The question that asked 'Why am I here?'" I interjected.

"Yes. The question is not a random one. It's one thing to glance at it; it's another to look at it and ask it of yourself… Your world will change. I know how it sounds. It's extreme, that's why we put a tip on the menu cover."

I was stunned, my situation was absurd - I was in a cafe, at midnight, without going to the village or the store, and the person in front of me was telling me that there was a life-changing revelation on the menu cover.

You don't find this kind of thing on a typical vacation. I didn't know it at the time. It was just the beginning, and there was so much more waiting for me that night.

Kayleen looked at me and said, "Look, John, once you actually ask that question, finding the answer becomes part of your life. You'll find that the first thought that comes to your mind when you wake up in the morning is that question. You'll have that question in your head now and then for the rest of the day. It's kind of like a door. Once you open it, it's hard to close again."

And I realized, "Why are you here?" And There is a deeper meaning, not what I thought when I first saw it. Through Kayleen's words, I understood that the question was not simply asking why people came to this cafe.

"That's right," Kayleen interrupted, "the question wasn't about the cafe, it was asking why a person exists."

I leaned against the back of the booth and looked around in shock. "What the hell is this place?" I thought to myself.

I tried to clear my mind: "Kayleen, I just wanted something to eat. What you said just now feels very eerie. If that door you just talked about and the thoughts that flashed through your mind every day are true, then why ask yourself this kind of question? I've never asked, and I'm fine now."

Kayleen put down the menu. "Really?" she asked. "Are you really fine?" She said "okay" with a hint of good-natured mockery, as if guiding me to explain what "okay" means. "Many people think 'good'. But some people are just looking for a more satisfying state, a better life than 'good'."

"So they came to this 'why cafe'?" I Said in a sarcastic tone.

"Some people are." Her voice was soft and calm. "Are you here for this?"

She turned the subject back. I don't know how to answer. I don't know why I'm here. I'm not even sure I know what this place is.

If I'm being honest with myself, I have to admit, I've wondered for years if there are more possibilities in life than what I've already experienced? I'm not saying life is bad. Of course, life can be frustrating, especially lately, but I have a decent job and close friends. Life is okay, even better. But I have a vague feeling in my heart that I can't explain it myself.

"It's because of that feeling that people ask that question," Kayleen said.

I was stunned. She speaks my mind again, and I realize she might be right. I took a deep breath and felt like I was on the edge of a cliff again. This time, I took a half step forward.

"Kayleen, can you tell me more about that question?"

She nodded. "I said just now that asking this question is like opening a door. It doesn't matter what words you use, whether it's a person's heart or soul. It will go after the answer. This question will occupy the priority of the questioner's life until he finds the answer one day."

"You mean, once someone asks himself 'Why am I here?' he can never let go. Is this the problem?" I asked.

"No, it's not impossible to let go. Some people just glanced at the question, maybe looked at it carefully, but in the end still forgot it. Some people asked themselves this question, and in a way really wanted to know the answer. They'll have a hard time ignoring it."

"Suppose someone asked this question and found the answer." I asked, "And then?"

"That's a good thing, and a very challenging one." She said with a smile.

"As I said earlier, the very act of asking a question creates the motivation to find an answer."

"If someone finds the answer, there's another force that's just as powerful. Once people know why they're here, why they're there, and they've found a purpose to live - they want to achieve it. That purpose is like a treasure map. The X on the top represents the location of the treasure. Once you see the X, it's hard to pretend you didn't see it, and it's hard not to go treasure hunting. Going back to the specific issue we talked about, once someone knows what they're here for, they get emotional from it. Physically, even physically, it's hard not to achieve that."

I leaned back, trying to appreciate everything Kayleen was explaining. "So asking a question will make it worse," I replied. "I'll just say it's better for people to never ask that question, get on with life, and don't open Pandora's box."

Kayleen looked at me: "Some people choose to ask. When the time comes, everyone has to ask themselves this question."

I didn't know how to react, so I laughed nervously. Thinking of how excited I was to see the streetlights when I lost my way, I don't know how to feel now.

"There are so many things to face," I said.

"I hope you don't feel like these things have to be 'faced', but 'welcome'," Kayleen responded. "You know what? The feeling you described before was not one that was told or described to you. Feeling. If one day you decide to let go of that feeling, just have the courage to make a choice, only you can decide for yourself."

After speaking, she stood up. "I have to leave and see how your special breakfast is going."

I had completely forgotten what breakfast I ordered. As soon as she reminded me, I slowly regained my senses. It turned out that I was still sitting in a cafe, still hungry.

My brain is spinning fast. I looked down at the menu and reread the first question.

Why are you here?

This question has a completely different meaning to me than when I first read it. I tried to recall Kayleen's previous words: "It's asking why a person exists."

I had a feeling that I couldn't put it into words, as if something was pulling me to ask that question. I remember talking to Kayleen and that question on the menu.

Why am I here?

I remember Kayleen saying what it would be like to take this seriously.

"It's crazy," I said to myself, rubbing my eyes. "I just want to eat something, some gas, and find a place to spend a few hours. Why should I think about those who don't have any? What?"

I drank half of the water in the glass, put it down, and found Jacob standing at my table with a large kettle in his hand.

"Do you want me to add more water?" he asked. "You seem to need a refill."

I accepted his offer, and he filled my glass with water.

"My name is Jacob," he said.

I stood up and shook hands with him. "Nice to meet you, Jacob. I'm John."

"Are you all right, John? It seemed as if you were lost in thought when I came over."

"Almost." I sat down again. "Kayleen just explained to me the line on the cover of the menu. I'm still trying to clear my mind and figure out what it means to me."

As soon as I finished speaking, I realized that Jacob might have a problem with me, and Kayleen knew nothing about the conversation just now. While he's the owner, the person who came up with that question and cover tip could also be Kayleen. Luckily, my words didn't confuse him in the slightest.

"Oh, that's not a simple question. Different people face it at different times. Some people figure it out when they're young, some don't figure it out until they're older, and some never figure it out their whole life. This phenomenon is actually quite interesting."

It seemed that Jacob understood the process of our conversation, and I confided my doubts to him.

"Jacob, Kayleen said, if a person asks this question to himself, his life changes a little." I pointed to the menu. "I wonder what will happen to them after that?"

Jacob glanced at the menu: " You mean after they ask a question? Or after they find the answer?"

I was stunned for a few seconds, considering his question. "Both. We talked a little about how a person finds the answer to a question, and what to do when he finds it. She just explained to me a bit about what it would be like to find the answer."

"Okay. Well, I don't think there's a one-size-fits-all approach to how to find answers. Everyone has their own way of living. However, I can tell you a few tricks that people I know have used to find their answers. "

I wanted to answer, but I didn't know what to say. My gut tells me that if I have some insight on how to find the answer to that question, it may be harder to avoid asking myself the question.

"That's true," Jacob said. "If it was Kayleen, she might tell you the same thing."

He seemed to know what I was thinking, even though I didn't say it at all. I'm just a little surprised by this.

The way others are looking for answers, I'm not sure I'm interested in knowing. After all, I wasn't even sure I wanted to ask that question.

"Jacob, what about another question? What will the person

who finds the answer do?"

Jacob laughed. "Well, I'll go see if your meal is ready first, and then come back and answer your question."

After a while, he returned with a tray full of plates. "Are these mine?" I asked. Could it be that there are two paragraphs below the set menu I ordered that I missed?

"Sure. A breakfast with omelets, toast, ham, bacon, fresh fruit, hash browns, biscuits, and pancakes on the side."

I looked around for three more people so we could eat together.

"Besides these, we have jelly with toast, syrup with pancakes, honey with biscuits, and a special potato salad for omelets. Thank you for being hungry John, you sometimes just don't realize that you're ready for new things."

Jacob put the meal on the table: "John, I have to talk to that couple over there. I'll be back in a while. If you still want to chat, we can continue."

"Okay." I looked at the plate in front of me. "No problem."

I dealt with the food on the table. Kayleen came when I ate some omelets, toast, and fruit.

"How's it going, John?" she asked as I was swallowing a piece of fruit.
"Good. Good. The breakfast was great." I told her."Good. Good. The breakfast was great."

The frustration that had engulfed me at the time was almost completely gone. My full attention was on the question, "Why are you here?" and I was fully engaged in the discussion that followed, and everything else became secondary. Having a delicious omelet helped me a little too.

"Do you want to eat by yourself? Or do you want someone to chat with?" Kayleen asked.

"Of course, I hope to join you. Actually, I want to continue the discussion with you. I've been thinking about it, but I'm still a little confused."

"Is there anything I can help explain?" Kayleen asked.

"I don't understand the question on the menu. If someone asks himself why he is here, somehow finds out his purpose, and he carries the answer, what is he going to do next?"

Kayleen paused: " First, he does what he wants. He solves the puzzle, and the answer belongs to him. They have a full, decisive say in what to do next."

I thought about it: "I think, if someone has come to this world with a purpose in mind, and they must want to know the best way to achieve it. The question is, where to find that way?" I looked at Kayleen and felt like she knew everything, but she was waiting for me to figure it out for myself.

"Everyone's approach is different."

I looked at her. "Can you give me a hint?"

"Maybe I'll give an example." She replied, "Suppose you want to be an amateur artist, what genre do you want to create? Works of art?"

I thought about it for a while. "I don't know. This question should depend on what kind of artist I want to be. Or simply create whatever I want." I stopped and waited for her evaluation, but she didn't say anything, so I had to think carefully about my answer just now.

"Is it that simple?" I asked. "If a person knows the meaning of his existence, will he do whatever he wants to achieve it?

"Something unique and important, and my body responded accordingly. This principle sounds too simple, so simple that people doubt its correctness. Do whatever you want to achieve your purpose.

"So, if my purpose in existence is to help others, then I

should do whatever I want, as long as it fits my definition of 'helping others'?" I asked excitedly, with a growing interest in the concept .

"That's right," Kayleen said. "If you think being in the medical profession can help others, then you go to practice medicine; if you think that building shelters in poor areas is to help others, then you go and build a house. Maybe you think that when an accountant, helping people with tax is your way of being meaningful, then be an accountant."

My mind was racing. I've never thought about things this way. In my past life, most of the decisions I've made have been in response to the expectations of others, such as family advice, cultural pressures, and other people's opinions. And now the problem is different. "And what if I exist to be a millionaire?"

"Then you should do whatever you can to do what fits your definition of a 'millionaire,'" Kayleen replied, "if that means to make other millionaires, go make them; if it means work hard and save a million, go work. All examples are one. The choice is yours."

"'*Make a million people rich*' I kind of like the phrase," I got more and more excited. "I could buy several new cars, maybe a few mansions."

"Is that what you exist for?" Kayleen lowered her voice.

Her question made me stop thinking immediately.

"I don't know."

"Jacob and I like to use an acronym when we talk about this," she said. "Like that question you glimpsed on the menu."

I looked down at the first question.

Why are you here?

"When a person finds out why he exists, it is equivalent to defining his own 'Purpose For Existing'. We call it 'PFE' for short. During a person's life, he can achieve 'Purpose For Existing'. 'Do ten, twenty, or even hundreds of things. He can do anything. Some of our clients are aware of their PFE and will try all kinds of activities that they think will help them achieve PFE, and these people are usually very interested in life. Satisfaction is high."

"Have you ever had a client with low life satisfaction?" I asked.

"These kinds of people do a lot of things, too," she said.

She paused, and I took the opportunity to say a thought that popped into my head: "But, what they're doing has nothing to do with their PFE." Kayleen smiled, and I realized that I had to come to this conclusion on my own.

"Kayleen, if I ask myself this question and I figure out my meaning, how do I know what to do to make it happen? I mean, the key to making meaning may be people, travel, activities, experiences or all sorts of other things. It's like finding a needle in a haystack."

She answered me with a question. I find her often answering questions with questions: "John, let's say you decide it's your life to know how to build a car, and you're ready to implement this PFE. What are you going to do next?"

I thought for a moment: "I should read a lot of books on cars. Maybe visit the factory where cars are made, get in touch with people who have experience building cars, get their opinions, and maybe get a job where they can actually assemble cars by hand."

"Will you always stay in the same place?"

I thought about it for a moment: "No, if I really wanted to know how to build a car, I would visit and study in different car-making places around the world, so that I could fully master the art of car-making. I think one needs to know how to realize one's own existence. Meaning, should explore and embrace all kinds of things related to PFE, and that's the answer to that question I asked."

"That's right," Kayleen said. "Everyone is limited to their current experience and knowledge. This sentence The emphasis is on 'now'. We live in the most informative age of all time, and everyone has access to all kinds of information, people, cultures and experiences around the world."

Kayleen continued: "As we strive to achieve PFE In the process, we have few external constraints, and the more constraints are imposed by ourselves."

"You are right." I said, "I don't seem to be taking full advantage of this era. Looking back on how I used my time, I realized that I was doing the same thing almost every day."

"Why?" she asked.

I looked down at the menu.

Why are you here?

"Maybe it's because I don't know the answer to this question," I said, pointing to the menu, "I don't know what I came into this world for or what I want to do, I'm just repeating what most people do."

"In your experience, does doing what 'most people' help you achieve your purpose?" she asked.

Kayleen's question went straight to my heart. Will doing what most people do help me to exist? Before I could answer, she spoke again.

"John, have you ever seen a green turtle?"

"Turtle?"

"Yes," Kayleen said, "a type of turtle. To be exact, a green turtle with green spots on its flippers and head. "

I think I've seen it in the pictures," I said. "What's wrong with this turtle?"

"It's weird to say," Kayleen began, "the most important lesson in my life was growing from a big green turtle." I learned it from the Turtles, and this lesson taught me what to do every day."

"What did it tell you?" I couldn't help laughing.

"It's interesting," she replied with a smile. "It didn't really 'tell' me anything, but it still taught me a lot. I was snorkeling on a Hawaiian beach at the time. It was a great day, I saw an eel with purple spots and an octopus, both of which I saw for the first time. I also saw thousands of fish, colorful, bright fluorescent blue, and the most dull crimson. You can just imagine it."

"Just 100 feet from the beach, I was diving next to some

huge rocks. I turned to the right and saw a large green turtle swimming beside me. It was the first time I saw a sea turtle in the wild. I was so happy that I quickly went up, took off the snorkel used for snorkeling, and floated on the water to observe it."

"I looked down and found it was right in front of me. Down below, swimming away from the shore. I decided to watch it in the water for a while. It flipped fins from time to time, but more often it just floated in the water. To my surprise, even though it seemed to swim slowly, I Still couldn't keep up with it. I was wearing fins that propelled me forward in the water. And I wasn't wearing a buoyancy vest or other gear that would slow me down. Even so, I was paddling hard to keep up, but still further and further away from it."

"About ten minutes later, it completely got rid of me. I didn't expect that I would not be able to keep up with a turtle. I was exhausted, disappointed, and a little embarrassed, so I had to turn back and snorkel and swim back to the shore."

"The next day, I went back to the same place hoping to see more turtles. I swam in the water for about 30 minutes and finally saw a group of small yellow and black fish, and another green turtle. It went around and I watched the coral for a while. I followed it as it swam deep into the ocean. Again, I was surprised to find that I still couldn't keep up with it. That's when it brought me to a valuable lesson."

Kayleen stopped here.

"Kayleen, you can't tell half the story. What does it teach you?"

She laughed: "I thought you didn't believe a green turtle could tell people anything."

I also laughed: " I was really skeptical about whether it could 'tell', but hearing this story here, I started to believe that it could indeed teach humans something. So what happened?"

"Later, I was floating on the water, and suddenly I found , the turtle's movements follow the motion of the sea. When the waves push toward the shore, in the opposite direction of the turtle's travel, the turtle will float up and paddle, but only to keep itself afloat. When the waves surge in the direction of the ocean , it will speed up the stroke so that it can ride the waves."

"The turtles never compete with the waves, but use the power of the waves. The reason I can't catch up with it is because I don't care about the direction of the water paddling all the way. At first, I was able to keep pace with the turtle, and sometimes had to slow down and wait for it. But in the opposite direction of the waves, the harder I swam, the more tired I became. When the waves were moving in the same direction as I was swimming again, I didn't have enough energy to move forward."

"As the waves came and went, I became more and more tired. The turtles always use the power of the sea to optimize themselves. That's why it swims faster than me."

"Kayleen," I said, "thank you for this great story about turtles..."

"Green turtles," she interjected with a smile.

"Well, the story of the green turtle. Everyone should love this good story about the green turtle, and so do I. And I love the ocean, maybe more than anyone else. But what does that have to do with how people enrich their lives? I don't know."

"You still don't understand, I had high hopes for you before." She smiled again.

"Okay, okay," I said, "let me think about it." I recalled our conversation before she told her story about the green turtle. Then I spoke again: "You're saying that if a person has figured out why he exists - and he knows his PFE, he can spend his time on things that help achieve PFE. You also say, no People who are PFE themselves also spend time doing a lot of things. So I come to the conclusion that they are spending their time on things that don't contribute to the realization of PFE."

"Good idea, I think you will quickly realize it makes sense," she said.

"Same." I said with a slight smile, showing that I caught her joking, "I think what the turtles… The green turtles taught you that if you're not on the same path as what you're trying to do, you're going to waste a lot of money and energy. By the time you get a chance to do what you want, you may not have the energy or time."

"Very good," she said, "Thank you for saying 'green turtle' instead of 'sea turtle'." She slightly restrained his smile: "That was a very important moment for me, definitely one of the 'just so' epiphanies in my life."

"Every day there are many people who want you to spend time and energy on them. Like the emails you get. If you're going to go to every event, every promotion, every unsolicited service, you don't have time to spare. It's just emails. Think about those People who want to get your attention through TV, the Internet, restaurants, travel, etc. You quickly find yourself doing what everyone else is doing, or what other people want you to do."

"After meeting the turtles the next day, I went back to the beach, full of new ideas. I sat on the beach towel and wrote them in my journal. In my life, those who tried to consume my attention, strength, energy and time, but the people, activities and things that are not related to my PFE are the reverse waves to the shore. And the people, activities and things that help me achieve PFE are the waves to the sea. So, the more time and energy I waste on reverse waves, the less time and energy I have left for positive waves."

"Once I figured that out, I saw things differently. I started to choose my 'paddling' moments carefully and focus on my reasons for 'paddling'."

"Interesting." I reflected on her story and started thinking about what I spent most of my day on. place, "I understand why you said the Green Turtle taught you a lesson."

"Kayleen, don't go yet, can I borrow a piece of paper and a pen from you?"

"Of course." She took a pen from his apron pocket, ripped a piece of paper from the order board, and put the two things on the table.

"You'll come up with an amazing answer," she said, blinking and leaving the table.

"How do you know?" I just asked her, but she had already gone to the kitchen.

I started writing numbers on paper. The average lifespan is 75 years...I was 22 when I graduated from college...I get emails 6 days a week...I spend 16 hours awake every day...I spend 20 minutes a day checking couriers and Email...

After doing all the calculations, I couldn't believe the answer I came up with. I did the math again and the result was the same.

I just realized that Kayleen wasn't exaggerating at all about the negative effects of reverse waves. Starting when I graduated college, and assuming a life expectancy of 75, I spent 20 minutes a day opening and browsing emails that I wasn't very interested in — a cumulative time that took up almost an entire year of my life.

I checked it three times, and the result was correct. I have about 53 years left after college, and one of those years will be wasted reading spam if I'm not careful.

"How's it going?" Kayleen came back from the kitchen, but I was so absorbed in the checking that I didn't notice her.

"You're right," I replied, "the results were amazing. Not only was I surprised, I was almost shocked. Who would have thought that just looking at spam could take an entire year of your life?"

She laughed. "John, not all mail is junk."

"I know, but at least for me, a lot of mail is really junk. And it's more than that. Emails have taken up my time and energy every day."

"I should really think about it," she said. "That's why I say that the green turtle deeply affected me." She smiled, turned and walked away towards another customer at the other end of the cafe.

12

I started eating pancakes that were just as delicious as any other meal, thinking back to my conversations with Jacob and Kayleen as I ate them. This kind of conversation doesn't happen in a normal cafe. Why do *you* exist? What do you do when you understand the meaning of your existence? What can you learn from a green sea turtle?

Just as I ate quite a bit of the fruit, Jacob walked up to my table.

"How is the food, John?"

"It's delicious, the food here is amazing. You should consider opening another branch, so you can make a lot of money."

Jacob smiled. "Maybe I've made a fortune already."

"Then why are you still working here..." I stopped hurriedly, but the words were already out of my mind, "Sorry Jacob, I'm not saying this cafe is bad, I mean... forget it. , I don't even know what I mean."

"It's okay," Jacob said, "I've been asked this question more than once. John, have you ever heard of a businessman who went on vacation and met a fisherman?"

"No. I've heard of it."

"That was a little story that was popular a few years ago," Jacob said. "Want to hear it? It's about your suggestion to open a branch."

"Yes, I want to hear it," I said.

"Okay. The story goes like this: a businessman went on vacation and wanted to get away from the hustle and bustle so he could save enough energy to make money again. He flew to a far-flung destination and wandered around a small village. A few days passed and he noticed the local there was a fisherman who seemed very happy and content. The merchant was very curious, so one day the merchant approached the fisherman and asked him what he was doing every day."

"The fisherman replied that he woke up every morning, had breakfast with his wife and children, then sent the children to school, and he went fishing, and his wife started painting. He would spend hours fishing. When there was enough fish for the whole family, he went back and took a nap when he got home. After dinner, he and his wife took a walk along the beach, watching the sunset; the children were swimming in the sea."

"The businessman was stunned. 'You Every day?'" he asked.

"'Basically,' replied the fisherman. 'Sometimes we do other things too, but most of the time we just do that. That is my life.'"

"'You catch fish every day?'" The merchant asked.

"'Yes,' answered the fisherman. 'There are a lot of fish in the sea.'"

"'Can you catch more fish than what you usually feed your family?'" the merchant asked.

"The fisherman smiled at him and replied: 'Yes, I often catch extra fish, but I let them all go. You see, I just like to fish.'"

"'But, why don't you catch them? Fish all day, catch as many as you can?' said the merchant, 'and then you can sell the fish and make a lot of money. Soon you'll be able to buy a second boat, a third boat, and hire other fishermen for you Catch more fish. In a few years, you'll be working in an office in a big city, and I bet you'll have an international fishing company in ten years.'"

"The fisherman smiled at the businessman again, 'Why would I do that?'"

"'To make money.' The businessman said, 'You can make a lot of money by doing this and then retire.'"

"'What will I do after I retire?'" asked the fisherman, still smiling.

"'You can do whatever you want, I think,'" said the businessman.

"'Like, having breakfast with my family?'"

"'Yeah, yes.'" said the businessman, a little annoyed that his idea did not excite the fisherman.

"'I like fishing. So if I retire, I can fish every day I want?'" the fisherman continued to ask.

"'Yes,' said the businessman. 'There were probably not as many fish back then, but there should be more or less.'"

"'Then at night I can walk along the beach with my wife and watch the sunset and our children swim in the sea?'" the fisherman asked.

"'Of course you can, do whatever you want, but your children should be grown up by then,'" said the businessman.

"The fisherman smiled and shook hands with the businessman, wishing him to work hard to make money as soon as possible."

After Jacob finished speaking, he asked me, "John, what do you think?"

"I think I am a bit like that businessman. When I have enough money to retire, I spend most of my time at work."

"I used to do the same," Jacob said, "and then I realized a very important thing. Retirement is the future, when I have enough money to do what I want. I can freely participate in activities I like, and arrange my daily life according to my own preferences. But one day, my work was particularly unsatisfactory. After work at night, I felt that I should live a better life. After a while, I found myself doubting the usual way of life. But it's unbelievable that this question is so taken for granted that I should have doubts, but I just can't figure it out."

As I listened to Jacob speak, While eating the food in front of him.

"I just realized that for me, every day is an opportunity to do what I want to do. Every day, I have an opportunity to answer that question on the back of the menu with action. I don't need to wait until 'retirement'. "

I put down my fork and leaned back. I was a little surprised that he said it so simply. "It's too easy," I said. "If it were that easy, everyone would have done what they wanted to do."

"But," Jacob said with a smile, "I'm afraid my situation doesn't apply to everyone. Personal. Take you, John, are you doing what you want?"

I didn't expect him to ask that. I secretly hope that Jacob will continue to talk, and I will continue to listen carefully. But I thought about it for a while.

"No, I don't." I replied.

"Why not?" The conversation went further and further in

unexpected directions. "To be honest, I don't know why. When I was in college, I actually didn't know what I wanted to study. There was one course I liked, and many people told me that people who study this major can find a job after graduation. So I decided to major. Then I graduated and started working, and my goal became to make more and more money. I got a job that paid well, and my life pretty much followed the same mode."

"I probably never thought about it." I pointed to the menu, "This is the first time tonight."

"I just said," Jacob said, "I don't know when and what this question will pass. It's a very interesting phenomenon."

"It's crazy," I said.

"What's crazy?"

"What we just talked about. Everyone can do what they want to do, but they spend so much time preparing for work instead of doing it right away. Why is this?"

" I think you should meet someone and she can share with you about this." Jacob got up and walked towards Kayleen who was talking to the other guests. I couldn't hear what they were discussing, but after a while, one of the guests got up and came up to me.

13

They walked over to my table and Jacob started introducing me to the woman he brought, "John, this is my friend Beth. Beth, this is John. Tonight is his first time at my cafe."

Beth laughed, smiled, and we shook hands.

"Nice to meet you," I said. "From Jacob's introduction, you should come here often for dinner, right?"

"Every once in a while," she replied, "It's a magical place, when you need it the most. Then you find yourself in it."

"I feel the same way," I said.

"Beth, John and I were just talking about one of your favorite topics, maybe we should hear from you since you're the expert."

She laughed, "Well, I don't know if I'm an expert, but I'm not. Lack of insight. What are you talking about?"

"John asked, why don't you do what you want to do right away, and spend so much time preparing for it."

"Ah, that's really my favorite. A topic to talk about." She laughed again.

Beth's laughter was contagious, and I immediately fell in love with her: "Beth, please take a seat. I want to hear your point of view. Jacob, if you have time, sit down and talk."

They are across from me. Taking a seat, Jacob said,
"Before I start this topic, let me briefly tell you about Beth.
She has an advanced degree from the world's top business
school and has been a well-known executive in advertising
for many years.

"Wow," I said, "I admire it."

"You're welcome," she responded with a smile, "but maybe
we can't get around this background when we talk about the
next topic. John, you watch TV, read magazines, surf the
Internet, or listen to Radio?"

"Sometimes," I said, "What's the matter?"

"Part of the answer to the question of why we spend so
much time preparing what we want to do, rather than just
doing it, lies in the information we receive every day," she
said. "Advertisers have long understood that if your By
targeting people's fears and desires directly, you can
motivate them to act. Once you find the right point of fear
or desire, you can drive them to buy a specific product or
service."

"Can you give me an example?" I asked .

"Okay. I don't know if you've seen or heard of an ad that's
focused on making you happy or making you feel safe, but
the message is, 'Only if you own this product, Your life will
be better.'"

"I don't know," I said, "there should be."

"These kinds of ads usually hide their true intentions very subtly," she said. "Most of the time, agencies don't express this directly. But if you are aware of the intent of the ad, or have been involved in the creation of many ads, you will find that the purpose of this information is to convince you that as long as you have a certain product or service, your life For example, driving this car will give your life special meaning, eating this ice cream will bring you happiness, and having this diamond will make you satisfied."

"And," she continued , "I'm going to tell you something very important. Advertising also has a more subtle, but more impactful message—that you get satisfaction from having those products, but if you don't have those products, Your life is not complete."

I looked at her suspiciously: "Beth, according to you, no one should buy anything. Your views are too extreme to be realistic."

"Oh , that's not what you mean," she replied. "You misunderstood. Anyone has the right to do what they want. I'm not saying you can't buy a car, go to the mall, or eat ice cream."

"Why do people spend so much time preparing instead of going straight to what they want to do? Part of the reason is that we are exposed to so much marketing every day, and if we're not careful, we're sure to put our own Happiness and satisfaction depending on a certain product or service. In the end, we end up in a financial quandary where we have to keep doing things to make money, even if those things aren't really what we want to do."

"I may not have understood. "I said.

"I'll give you a very general example," Beth said. "This example doesn't apply to everyone, but it helps to clarify what we've just discussed."

"From childhood, our lives are filled with various Advertisements, the message of these advertisements is that the fulfillment of life comes from material things. In this case, what will we do? Of course it is for shopping. We buy the products in the advertisements to see if the advertisements are true. Here comes the problem," she continued. "It takes money to buy goods. To earn money, I have to find a job. This job may not be our ideal, and the time I spend at work may not be my ideal. Timing, but with this job I can afford what I want. I told myself this situation is temporary. It won't be long before I can start doing other things - closer to me What I originally wanted."

"There is another problem, because I have done an unsatisfactory job and spent a lot of time on it, I will feel more and more dissatisfied. There are many people around us who are looking forward to it all day long. When we retire, they always say that when we retire, we can do what we want to do. Before long, we ourselves will be looking forward to this almost deified future. When we retire, we will no longer have to work. Instead, you can spend your time doing what you want to do."

"We don't do what we want to do every day. To make up for the emptiness in our hearts, we buy more things. We hope that the advertisements are true, even if only a little bit of it is true, and hope that those goods can replace the daily work. Gives us satisfaction. But unfortunately the more we buy, the more we have to pay, the more time we need to work to pay for everything. The time we spend working is not Inwardly, so the more time we put into our work, the more dissatisfaction we get, because we have less time for what we really want to do."

"And then we buy more stuff," I said, " I see the logic. It's not a virtuous cycle."

"Whether it's a virtuous cycle," Beth said, "the end result is long hours, busy doing things that don't achieve PFE. They keep saying, ``I'm looking forward to the future, hoping that one day they won't have to work and can live their lives as they want."

"Wow, I've never thought about it that way." I said, "Is it really?"

Beth and Jacob laughed . "John, I don't recommend you take the advertisement seriously, I hope you can see the essence through the phenomenon; in the same way, I don't want you to accept my statement without doubt." Beth replied, "Kayleen just said, now Everyone has the opportunity to come into contact with more new things and learn about all things in the world. What I share is just the words of my family. After listening, you can observe the world with your own eyes and judge whether what I said is partially true, all true, or not at all. "

Well, your words gave me a new perspective to see things." I said, "Beth, have you experienced the example you just gave?"

Beth laughed: "You must have experienced it. Now say I could joke about it when I got up, but I didn't think it was funny at all. I was really unhappy and felt like I couldn't control my life. Every day I worked long hours and didn't have much free time; Reward yourself. I thought it was a very reasonable way of life at the time."

"I'm also working on weekends, so I say to myself, I should reward myself with a new outfit, the latest electronics, or some new fashion piece of furniture. But since I'm always working, I rarely have time to enjoy my Reward myself with these things. My friends who come to my house say they love the style of my house, but I don't have time to enjoy it at home."

"One night, I was just going through a lot of bills, and they looked as usual. , devoured most of my monthly income. I lay flat on my bed, staring at the ceiling, the only way to keep myself from crying. I found myself missing out on most of my life, wasting it on a job I didn't care about At work, I use shopping to comfort myself. To be honest, I don't even care about the things I buy."

"I want to find out how I got here. My original plan in life was to work until Sixty years old, you can't do what you want until you retire. I feel sorry for myself."

"But your mentality is completely different now." I said, "What have you been through?"

Beth replied with a smile : "My mentality is really completely different now. I thought about it for a while that night and decided to go out to relax. I live in a big city and there are always people coming and going on the streets. I look at everyone who passes by me, curious. Are there any of them who feel the same way as I do?"

"Are they happy? Are they doing what they want? Are they content? Finally, I stopped in front of a small coffee shop. I've been to this shop several times but never been in. Surprisingly, an acquaintance of mine sat in the shop. I met him a few times on different occasions and was very impressed because he was always there and every time he looked calm."

"He invited me to sit with him. We drank a few cups of coffee and talked about life for three hours. I described my state to him, and he smiled and pointed out that I might have watched too much of my ad. I didn't quite understand what he meant. So he told me about the cycle I just told you about, and he told me something else that I still remember clearly."

"'The whole point of changing your mindset is,' he said, 'you have to be clear that whether something makes your life more complete is up to you and has nothing to do with people telling you it's not complete.'"

"That day I came home in the evening, sat down and started thinking, what kind of life is perfect for me, and why. I forced myself to think about how I would like to spend my days. After a while, I asked myself again… Why do I want to spend each day like that? In the end, my mind led me to this question," she said.

I looked down and Beth was pointing at the menu.

Why are you here?

"Then what?" I asked.

Beth laughed again: "Kayleen may have told you that once you ask yourself why you're here, your world changes. I'm not going to nag about the boring details, but I can tell you that since then When it's too late, I'm not who I was."

"My life started to change from small things, I started to set aside a little more time for myself each week. I no longer needed 'material' rewards for hard work. Instead, start doing what I want to do. Every day, I spend at least an hour doing something I really enjoy. Sometimes, I read a novel that makes my blood boil; sometimes, I go out for a hike or do Exercise."

"Then one hour turned into two hours, and two hours turned into three hours. When I came back to my senses, I'd focused all my energy on the things I wanted to do that made 'me Why are you here?' The answer to that question comes to fruition."

14

Beth turned her head and asked Jacob, "Have you discussed death?"

"What?" A sudden unease passed through me.

Beth smiled and pointed to the menu: "Second question."

I looked down.

Are you afraid of death?

I almost forgot there were two more questions on the menu. After delving into the first question, I'm not sure if I'm ready to think about other questions.

"These issues are interrelated," Jacob said.

He guessed my mind again! It's a shame that I thought this was a normal cafe just now, but from the very beginning, I thought this place was a little different. "What's up with 'interconnectedness'?" I asked.

"Are you afraid of death?" Beth asked. "Most people are. It's one of the most common human fears."

"I'm not sure," I replied. Haven't experienced everything I want to do and don't want to die yet. But I don't think about my own life or death all day."

"Anyone who hasn't asked themselves these questions, no one who has worked hard to achieve PFE," Beth looked at me One glance, and then a pause, "These people are afraid of death."

I was at a loss for words and looked at Beth and Jacob: "You mean, most people think about death every day? I can't believe it. At least I don't stay all day. Thinking about death."

Jacob smiled: "No, that's not what we mean. Our statement is more focused on the subconscious of people. Most people don't have a clear concept of death in the things they think about every day. But as time goes by, People live in this world, and they have less and less time left to do what they want to do. Everyone's subconscious is very clear that death is approaching. Therefore, they are afraid that one day in the future, they will never have a chance. They are afraid that death will come. that day."

I thought a little bit about what he just said. "It's not necessarily what you said? If someone finds out the meaning of their existence, chooses what they want to do, realizes their PFE, and finally does it, why should such a person be afraid of death? If you have achieved Wishes, or doing what you want to do every day, there is no reason to be afraid of losing the opportunity to do those things."

Beth smiled. "That's it," she said softly, standing up. "John, it's nice to meet you and chat with you. But I have to go back to my friend."

I also stood up and shook her hand. "Nice to meet you, too," I said, "thank you for sharing your insights with me."

She turned and walked to the previous table, and I slipped back to my box. I feel a change in myself. I don't know exactly what the change is, but what I've just learned must be very important for a long time in my life.

Jacob stood up. "John, are you alright? You seem to be a little overwhelmed."

"I was just thinking," I replied, "that you and Beth are saying very well. I'm surprised I hadn't heard it before, I didn't think about those questions."

"Let it be, John. You may have had these thoughts before, but you weren't ready to actually accept them and practice them."

Jacob reached out and picked up two empty plates from the table: " Let me help you clear the table. Do you still have hash browns?"

"You still have, it's delicious." I said, pulling my mind back to the food in front of me, "These things are delicious. I'm still hungry, but I can't let you take them away."

Jacob left the table and I focused again, thinking about the conversation he, Beth, and I had just had. There is so much to digest. I think back to Beth's story and the impact the ad had on people. How much of my definition of success, happiness and fulfillment is influenced by others? It's also hard for me to tell. I have decided to be cautious about the deep messages behind people's words from now on.

The discussion of death is another matter entirely. After we finished talking, I had a deeper understanding of death. I don't live in despair and anxiety about death all the time; in fact, I rarely think about death. But living a life of fulfilling my purpose and seeing each day in a different light resonated immensely deep in my soul.

"If you've done what you want to do, or are doing what you want to do every day, there's no reason to be afraid of losing the opportunity to do it," I said to myself.

I wish I had thought about it or heard about it. "However," I thought, "it's not enough to know the idea, the important thing is to actually do it."

15

I looked down at the menu again.

Why are you here?

Are you afraid of death?

Are you satisfied?

These problems don't seem so strange compared to when I first saw them. In fact, they are now extremely important issues.

Are you satisfied?

"You can only be satisfied when you figure out why you exist and start making a real effort to be there for that meaning," I meditated.

"It's not easy, is it?" Kayleen asked.

When I looked up, I saw her reaching for my water glass. "Yeah, it's not easy," I said, "I'm thinking about my own situation. I know how to do my job well, that's my way of making a living. If I ask myself why I exist, and figure out what I want to do, What do I do when I find I don't know what to do? What if I can't find a job related to my goals? How do I make money?"

"How do I support myself, how do I save for retirement? What if I can't do a good job in my new job? What if the things I want to do are laughed at or looked down upon?"

Kayleen waited for me to finish before speaking: "John, if a person thinks about why he exists step by step , found the answer to this question, do you think they'd be excited by what they found?"

"And then, wouldn't it be exciting to do something that makes sense?" she asked.

I was stunned again. This question seems a little simpler. Did I miss it? "Of course the answer is yes," I said, "how can he not be excited? In this case, no matter how excited a person is, no matter how motivated he is."

"Then do you think there is any reason for this person to fail? ?"

I looked at her. Before I could answer, she spoke again.

"Have you seen people who go all out to do things every day? Do they spend their time doing things that they can really enjoy?"

I thought about it and said, "There aren't many of them, but I do Know a few."

"Are they good at what they love?" Kayleen asked.

"Of course they're good at it," I replied with a hint of sarcasm. "They spend a lot of time on those things, and of course they're good at it. For example, the books they read in their spare time are about those things, the TV they watch. The show is about those things, and even going to the rallies...with that input, they're sure to be good at what they do."

"Are they going to get bored?" she asked.

"No," I said, "they don't seem to be doing enough of what they love to do. These kinds of people act like they've been beaten, and..." I stopped halfway through.

Kayleen smiled at me: "Do you think it would be difficult for this type of person to find a job?"

I thought about it: "The people I know certainly have a hard time finding a job. They not only have a lot of knowledge about what they like to do. , and they do it with enthusiasm, people like to consult them about things, and they like to get them to do things together."

"I can imagine that they must be very positive and optimistic." She said, "Maybe they don't need to travel far away at all. , you can keep yourself motivated all the time."

I thought about Kayleen's words for a while. It's very interesting to look at things from this angle. What would my life be like if I kept doing what I wanted to do? What if my time was always spent on the things I was willing to give my best to? "What about the money?" I asked. "They're just good at something, and they know a lot about something, but that doesn't mean they make a lot of money. They can get a job anytime, but will it pay well?" "I feel better when I ask that question. "After all," I continued, "what one does to be satisfied, who knows?"

"I see what you mean," Kayleen said. "In terms of money, we might as well imagine a worst-case scenario. A person who finds something that fits his purpose of existence, does it every day, and still uses it. And yet he couldn't make 'a lot' of money. Omg, what a tragedy."

"Imagine the consequences of doing that. Your lifestyle aligns with your PFE and you can spend your life doing what you want. because you've figured out your meaning. But... by the time you're 65, you may find that you haven't saved enough for retirement."

"So what do you do?" she asked in exaggerated sarcasm. "I guess it's tragic that you can only keep doing the things you want to do."

I laughed: "Kayleen, if you want to be sarcastic, just say it."

She responded with a smile: "I just wanted to Express, I totally understand what you're thinking."

"I get it, I get it, and the question goes back to Jacob's fisherman story. Why wait when you can do what you want now?"

"Yes, but More than that. Do you remember the conversation you had with Beth? You talked about why some people like to buy things."

"Certainly remember, we said that some people buy more things to make more money. They want to satisfy themselves by shopping. , because what they are doing every day is not what they really want to do. But there is a trap, the more things they buy, the longer they work to make money, and if they are not careful, they will fall into a vicious circle."

I stopped and realized that this was the part I didn't fully understand. Kayleen and I looked at each other. "It's about the worst outcome you just said, isn't it?" I asked. Kayleen nodded.

I thought for a while: "First of all, I think the worst offenders can choose to do other things."

Kayleen nodded again, and I continued.

"That's the worst possible outcome, and there's obviously a slightly better outcome. It's that a person can do what he wants to do, and he can achieve his purpose and make a lot of money at the same time."

Kayleen nodded again.

I know I haven't fully figured it out yet. I leaned back in my chair and took a sip of water. I was just about to ask Kayleen to give me a hint when a thought popped into my head: "Maybe it won't matter if you have money or not. It depends on the person and his circumstances. However, think back to my conversation with Beth. , I remember saying I didn't understand, why do people work in the end?

My discussions with Beth turned out that people work in part because they seek satisfaction from work."

"Can you give an example?" Kay Akane asked.

"For example, I work to earn money," I replied. "I need to buy things. I think back on the things I bought, and I feel like I'm a bit like the kind of person Beth was talking about. The things I have can take me away. Being realistic for a moment relieves my stress and makes me feel better."

"But I wonder, if I don't need 'escape' or 'decompression', would I still want to buy those things? If I've been doing what I want to do, then I should have nothing to 'escape' and less stress to release. I'm not saying I'm going to build a house in the mountains and forests, I just want to know, what's wrong with a person's 'a lot of money' Will the definition of ' change because of the degree to which he achieves PFE?"

Kayleen nodded again: "So you don't think people should aspire to have more money?"

"No." I carefully organized the words in my heart. I want to express my thoughts clearly.

"That's not what I meant. I'm just talking about it from my own perspective. I feel like if I figured out why I exist and started doing things that I thought would achieve my goals, then maybe I wouldn't take it as seriously as I do now. Money. That's what I mean."

Kayleen got up and took the two empty plates from my table. She smiled. "John, you have an interesting idea."

I watched her head to the kitchen.

"Yes this place is interesting."

16

Kayleen came back and added some water for me, then sat down across from me. "John, when I was sending your cutlery back to the kitchen just now, Jacob reminded me that there is a topic you might be interested in. We just said that there are all kinds of challenges people can face in their efforts to achieve PFE, the topic is about those challenges."

"Like the one I asked—how do they make money?"

"That's just one of them, there are many."

I looked at Kayleen and said, "Tell me, I want to hear it. ."

"Just to be clear," she began, "you think about the people we talked to before."

"You mean my friends who went all out to work?" I asked, "really enjoying every person for a day?"

"Yeah. Do you see any difference between them and others?"

"Well, there's a woman in sales who's in..."

"Wait," Kayleen interrupted, "Don't Just think about what they do, think about the big picture, and think about the characteristics of their group."

I leaned back in my chair and closed my eyes. I had a picture of those people in my head: "Okay, I said, they all seem to have a kind of visceral joy, they all enjoy what they do. The impression of bravado. They all have a plan, as if they think things are going to go their way."

"And it may sound a little strange, but another characteristic of people like them is that they are lucky. Good things happen to them all the time. , and unexpected."

"Can you give me an example?" Kayleen asked.

"Okay, let's take the woman I was talking about. Coincidentally, like Beth, she's also in advertising. She needs to get a big client. I don't know what the situation is, but I remember that it involved a large order, many people have fought for, but they have all failed."

"However, she was determined to take the order. She spent two weeks preparing materials for presentation to the client, and then got a call from a college classmate. She and this person have not been in touch for a long time. When talking about work, she said that she was trying to win a big client. As a result, her college classmate had a friend who happened to be an employee of the big client company she was trying to win."

"After a few phone calls, the three of them met for a meal. Supper. A few weeks later, she signed this big client for granted. So I say, good things always happen unexpectedly to these types of people. They're just lucky."

"John, why do you think they're lucky? ' Kayleen asked.

I took a few sips of water: "I don't know, maybe it's just a coincidence. But there's an interesting phenomenon, I think about people who really enjoy doing things, they spend their time on things that are consistent with PFE, And this kind of great thing always seems to be encountered by them."

Kayleen smiled and looked at me: "Can this kind of thing only be encountered by them? Have you ever encountered it?"

I leaned against the back of the booth : "Should have. I can't think of specific examples for a while, but I remember a few times when the surprise came just when I needed it."

"John, if you can think of those specific examples, you're sure You'll find a connection between the two."

"For example, when the surprise happened, I happened to be doing what I wanted to do?" I asked. As soon as the words came out, my whole body was shaken, and I felt exactly the same as I had before, which is how I felt when I had a major discovery related to myself.

"John, I can't answer this question for you. But I work in this cafe and watch the guests come and go, and I have a discovery - those who know their PFE, those who go all out to achieve PFE, they Very lucky indeed. There are always surprises when they need it most.”

"I asked some of them about this phenomenon, and they felt the same way, but they didn't know the reason behind it, and they gave different explanations. In fact, most of them didn't care about their luck at all. They just know that lucky coincidences come naturally when they are striving for the meaning of existence, and they call it letting the flow take its course."

"It's weird," I said, "it sounds a little mysterious."

"Some people think that Xuan, some people think it is the natural law of the universe, and some people think that there is a stronger force behind it. However, most people just think that this is luck. Everyone agrees that this is the case, and luck is indeed one of the factors that makes things work."

"What do you think, Kayleen?"

She thought for a while: "I don't know either. It could be the reasons mentioned above, or it could be another reason. Have you ever tried exponential theory?"

"No, can you explain it?"

"Yes, this theory is actually very simple. Let me give an example, if you tell someone a piece of news, he will tell the news to other people, and other people You'll tell more people. It won't take long for your message to reach a lot of people, better than if you could tell them one by one. That's exponential theory."

"It's kind of like emailing," I said, " You send an email to 10 people, each of them forwards it to 10 other people, and it goes on and on."

"That's right. That's one thing. Now let's get back to the point, if you tell everyone you're working on it. To achieve your PFE, you share the news with 10 people, and they each share it with 10 other people, and it won't take long for you to have a large group of potential helpers."

I thought for a while: "But why should they? Willing to help me? Why should my friend talk to other people about what I'm trying to do?"

Kayleen looked at me and didn't answer. I feel like she's encouraging me to find out for myself again. I thought about our conversations, and thought about how we talked about indices. But I couldn't come up with an answer: "I don't get it, Kayleen, can you give me a hint?"

"John, think about the people we just mentioned -- people who work to achieve their PFE, you and them. Do you feel anything while interacting?"

"It feels great, I can't help being touched by their passion and enthusiasm, and I want to take the initiative to help them."

I paused: "No, Kayleen, don't tell me this. That's the answer! What about the messaging example?"

"John, you said that their passion and enthusiasm make you want to help too. If you can't help, but know that others might be able to, you Would you contact them?"

"Of course I would, I would feel motivated to do it because they..." I paused, figuring out how to express it.

"On the right path?" Kayleen prompted.

"Yeah, that's about it. They're on the right track, and you can't help but want to help."

"Then what do you say when you talk about them to the person who might be able to help? ?" Kayleen asked.

I smiled half to myself and half to Kayleen. "I'll be like them, speaking with passion and enthusiasm. The topics will be contagious, as if their stories or needs carry a positive emotion with them."

"Maybe this is the answer you're looking for." Kayleen Station Get up and start clearing the tableware. "John, you've eaten so much," she said, holding a stack of empty plates. "Are you starving?"

"Your food is so delicious," I replied, "I don't want any leftovers. .."

I glanced at the kitchen and saw Jacob. We waved to each other, not feeling anything strange this time: "Kayleen, I want to ask, do you still have strawberry rhubarb pie?"

She laughed: "I'll go to the kitchen and ask."

17

After a few minutes, Jacob came to my table with a plate with enough pie for four. "You ordered a strawberry rhubarb pie?" he asked.

"Jacob, why is the portion so big? I don't know if I can finish it."

He put down the plate and put a new napkin and a new fork on the table: "Eat slowly, don't worry. You and Kayleen: How was the chat?"

I just forked a large piece of pie and put it in my mouth, munching on it. Hearing this, I quickly took a sip of water and swallowed the pie: "It was a good chat, very interesting. We talked about people who asked themselves this question in a different way." I said and pointed to the menu.

In an instant, the question on the menu changed to "Why am I here?", and then slowly back to "Why are you here?" This time I didn't ask him about the change at all.

"Yeah, that's the question," I continued. "Those people seem to have something in common, like they all know why they exist, they know what to do to achieve that meaning, and they're completely confident in their abilities. They try to. There was always divine help in the process, and it went very smoothly. Kayleen explained some related theories to me."

Jacob grinned: "Everyone's speculation about this phenomenon can be traced back to a long time ago, even back to the earliest philosophical Home."

"Jacob, there's something I don't quite understand. Why doesn't everyone go after their own PFE? What's the problem with them? Don't rush to answer, I know I should ask myself first, actually, you come over here. I was thinking about it. But I'm really curious if there's an answer that's bigger and applicable to more people than I might have come up with myself."

Jacob took a sip of his mug and took a sip. , then put the cup on the table and sat down across from me. "Each of us has our own answers to that question," he began to explain. "These answers are for ourselves because each person's situation is unique. There are, however, a few larger determinants."

"For example?"

"Many people have never thought about the meaning of their existence. Some people have thought about this concept, but they don't know if they have the so-called PFE. Some people don't think of themselves because of their upbringing environment or religious beliefs. have the right to pursue and achieve their own PFE."

"Some people feel that they have a meaning to exist and believe they have the right to achieve that meaning. But even so, some people don't think that they can achieve PFE just by believing in themselves and doing it. , they don't believe the process is that easy."

"It goes back to what you were talking about with Beth. There are many people who, for money or power, convince others that their product or service is the key to a fulfilling life. .Imagine if everyone realizes that our satisfaction is really in our own hands, the kind of people in front of them will be greatly threatened. Those who persuade others will lose their power. For these kinds of people, losing the right Other people's influence is not a good thing."

"You reminded me of what Kayleen and I just said." I said, "She told me that if people figure out their PFE, they will do what they want to do. to become whoever you want to be, without the permission or consent of others."

"That's right. What's more, this way no one can stop or arrange for others to do what they want. Everyone can control their own destiny."

I thought about it and recalled the conversation I had with Kayleen and Beth just now: "The situation you are talking about is very different from what I usually see and hear. Finding meaning in one's own existence and taking control of one's own destiny is difficult for many people to touch, let alone follow up on and actually live."

"It's hard," Jacob said, "but it's not impossible. In fact, just a few weeks ago, a guest came to the café and told Kayleen and me a very interesting story about how he learned to take control of his own destiny. I can tell you if you're interested.

" All right. Is there a fisherman in the story?"

Jacob laughed: "Not this time, but there are sports. This guest has been dreaming for years that he is going to hit a very hard golf ball. He said he is not good at golf in real life, but he is not good at golf in his sleep. It was very frustrating to encounter such a problem. In the dream, the ball he was about to hit was either on the window frame, or on a large rock slope, or in some other absurd and difficult place.

" Every time he tried to get on his feet and practice his swing, it never felt right, and he knew he was going to hit a bad shot. As a result, the more he practiced his swing, the more anxious he became."

"Wait for him. The depression peaked and he finally felt ready. As a result, every time he was about to swing, the ball would change to a new, equally difficult position. Then he had to go through A new wave of stress and anxiety. It kept repeating until he woke up from the dream with his heart beating wildly and his muscles tense."

"He had the dream again one night, but this time, when he couldn't. When he was even more frustrated, he suddenly realized that he could just pick up the ball and play it elsewhere. There was no super problem, no one cared where he hit the ball except himself."

"He said, after waking up , he had an unbelievably strong feeling—he felt like he had insight into a deep truth. He didn't know it before, but now he sees it so clearly. At the end of the conversation, he told me, 'No matter what people tell us to believe, No matter what we hear in the advertisements, no matter how we feel about the high pressure of work, each of us can grasp every moment in our life. I forgot this before, so under the influence of various external forces, I was always trying to adjust myself and I was unknowingly being controlled by them.'"

"'No one cares where I hit the ball except myself; by the same token, in life, only you truly know what you mean by being there. Never Losing control of your own destiny because of other people or events. Actively choose your own life path, or you will have to accept the arrangement passively. Learn to remove the golf ball in your life.'"

Jacob finished the story, looking at me Said, "Look, there really is no fisherman."

"The story has no fisherman, and it's brilliant. I like the message that the story contains."

"The guest also liked it. He said the dream changed his life. After that, he realized that he could do something about his own destiny. Choice. Now, if something happens that he doesn't know how to do, he tells himself to remove that golf ball. He says that as long as he says that, he will no longer be afraid and will have the courage to do whatever he wants."

18

I looked at my watch, it was five fifteen in the morning. "No way," I said. "I'll be able to order breakfast again soon."

Jacob smiled. "Let's finish your pie first."

"Then I'm welcome," I replied. , and put a fork full of food into his mouth. I took another sip of water after eating, "Jacob, there's something I don't understand. I've talked to you and Kayleen about this, but I still haven't found an answer."

Jacob smiled and said, "Then ask me . But I can't tell you the recipe for the strawberry rhubarb pie, it's one of the few secrets we have here. The recipe was passed down to me by my mom, and I swore to her never to tell anyone."

I grinned. "Got it. Thankfully I'm asking a different question. We've discussed people asking themselves 'Why am I here?' Kayleen and I have also discussed the impact of that question on the questioner, and people What can I do when I know the answer. But there's one thing I don't understand..."

"How to find out, eh?" Jacob asked.

"Yes."

"I think it's better to call Kayleen over to answer this

question. She and I answer you better than me or she alone." So Jacob got up and walked to the other end of the cafe. Kayleen was sitting there chatting with Beth and her friends. I don't know if they are talking about similar topics.

After a while, Kayleen got up and walked towards me with Jacob.

"Is the pie good?" Kayleen asked when they were both seated.

"It's delicious," I said with a grin. "I'm almost full."

"Kayleen, John wants to know how to find the answer to the first question." Jacob said, pointing to the "You Why am I here", the question now becomes "Why am I here", "I think it's best for both of us to answer his question."

Kayleen nodded, looked me straight in the eyes, and asked in a very serious tone, "John, do you have a mailbox?"

"Yes."

"After you ask yourself that question, on the seventh day of next month, On the day of the first full moon, you'll get a package in your mailbox. There's a document in it. You hold it up, look by candlelight, and you'll see a secret message written by someone who knows the answer. You can only read a message once in your life, you can only see it by candlelight, and you must read it on the seventh day of the month."

I put down the water glass and leaned over to listen to her carefully.

"This package is very recognizable, the outer packaging is made of red ribbon, tied with a double knot, which..."

At this time, I noticed that the table was moving, or more like it was shaking. I straightened up.

"What's the matter, Kayleen?" I asked in surprise. "The table..."

Kayleen continued, as if unaware that the table was shaking. "The big rope loop is at least twice as long as the small rope loop, and it's tied to the upper left corner of the package."

I glanced at Jacob, surprised and embarrassed, because the shaking of the table was not haunted, but caused by Jacob. While listening to Kayleen talking, he lay on the table with his mouth covered, trying his best to hold back his laughter. But he laughed so hard that his whole body was shaking, and the table was shaking.

I laughed. Kayleen turned and gave Jacob a playful thump on the shoulder.

"Your acting is really bad," she said with a smile.

"Sorry," Jacob said, "you're talking too much like that. I just can't help myself."

"Okay," Kayleen said, "John, I'm a little freer about the answer you're looking for. A bit."

"A little bit!" Jacob said, "you're just making it up. What's the 'double knot...'" Jacob imitated Kayleen, and the three of us laughed again.

"You're really good at making up stories, Kayleen," I said. "But you haven't answered my question yet."

"That's what makes it interesting," she said, grinning, "I did it to make a point. Some people realize the problem and want to know the answer, but they just want to find the answer under the guidance of someone else or something."

"Like a package received on the seventh day." I continued with a smile.

"Yeah, day seven. But the point is, we have our free will to decide what we want to do when we have the answer, and by the same token, we can take our own initiative to find

the answer." "So, you mean, "I said, "You can't just take the first step and just stand there and wait. If someone really wants to know why he exists, he has to find out for himself."

"Yes," Jacob said. "People look for The answer varies. Some people ask themselves why they exist through meditation; some people listen to their favorite music while recording their thoughts; many people choose to be alone in nature; Friends or strangers communicate and share this topic; others will read, guided by the ideas and stories in the book to find out."

"Which method works best, and do you have any suggestions?" I asked.

Kayleen turned to me and said, "John, it's all about the individual. You have to remember one key point, our answers, only we in the world can decide. So many people choose to be alone in the process of searching for answers. "

I can understand that," I said. "When you're bombarded with information and information all day long, it's hard to focus and think."

"Yeah," Jacob responded. "Someone spends time meditating, or going out to nature." Quiet and quiet, usually to escape the 'noise' of the outside world and focus on what you really want to think about."

"Is that the whole answer?" I asked.

"Not all," Kayleen said. "John, do you remember when we talked about the value of being exposed to different ideas, cultures, perspectives, people, etc.?"

"Remember, of course, when we were talking about why a person needs to know more about different things in order to realize his meaning."

"That's right," Kayleen said, "and the same point applies to those looking for PFE. Some people find that once they have a new experience or come into contact with a new idea, some experience or idea will resonate with them. When encountering something they love, many people have a physiological reaction, such as standing hair, electric shock to the spine, and tears of joy. Wait. Others have a 'it's it' feeling. These are clues to finding the meaning of their existence."

"I see," I laughed, "I had that feeling too. When I read Or when I hear something, it's very clear in my heart that I just want to do it. In fact, I've felt that way several times tonight."

Kayleen smiled at me: "John, your question. Have you solved it?"

"It should be. If I understand correctly, you are saying that there is no one-size-fits-all answer, but you can try to find a place to concentrate on the problem. To experience different things, to be exposed to different ideas, Paying attention to how we react to various things helps us find answers."

"Yes," Jacob said.

Kayleen stood up: "I'm going to see the other guests. John, do you need anything else?"

"No, Kayleen, thank you. But in case I get an unexpected gift on a full moon night— —The package with the red ribbon...I might ask you a few more questions."

She laughed and winked at Jacob: "No problem, feel free to ask questions."

19

Kayleen left my table. "John, where were you going before you came here?" Jacob asked.

"I just started my vacation. I feel like I need to take some time out, get away from everything, and think about it. I don't know exactly what I want to think about, but just now..." I glanced at my watch, "...just now During the eight hours I spent, I came up with some pretty good ideas."

"Jacob, do you mind if I ask you a personal question?"

"Don't mind, what question?"

I looked at him: "What's your motivation? , put these questions on the menu?"

Jacob leaned back in his chair with a small smile on his face: "How did you know there was an opportunity?"

"Because of you, your behavior, and this place. I'm not sure, but I feel like you're doing what you want. So I guess you asked yourself that question, and this cafe is your answer."

Jacob smiled again, took a sip from the mug and said : "Many years ago, I lived an extraordinarily busy life. I had grad classes at night and a full-time job during the day. The rest of the time I spent every minute of my physical training with the goal of becoming a professional athlete.

For two years Almost every time slot in my life was full for half the time."

"After graduation, I quit my job to give myself a summer vacation, because I had found a new job and officially joined in early September. A buddy of mine also Having just graduated, we decided to take a trip to Costa Rica together to celebrate graduation."

"We spent weeks wandering around the country, hiking in the rainforest, observing wildlife, and immersing ourselves in a whole new cultural environment. One day, we sat On a stretch of driftwood, eating fresh mangoes and watching the waves crash on an incredible beach. We did body surfing in water close to 30 degrees Celsius for an entire afternoon. At sunset, we were in a relaxed mood, watching the sky go from Bright blue to pink, orange, and then red."

"Sounds spectacular," I said.

"Indeed. I remember looking at the beauty in front of me and starting to think back. For the past two and a half years, I lived according to plan every moment, and this beauty appeared every day. It turned out that it only took a few hours to fly and then walk. It's a few dirt roads to heaven, but I didn't even know it existed. I found that during my crazy two and a half years, not only was this place always there, the sun was always there, and the waves were always washing over it. A beach, everything in front of me has existed for millions of years, even hundreds of millions of years."

"Thinking of this, I feel very small. My troubles, my stress, my worries about the future, it seems that nothing matters. In my previous life, no matter what I did or didn't do, whether my decision was right or wrong, or a mixture of right and wrong, even if I am gone one day in the future, the scenery in front of me will still exist for a long time."

"I sat there, facing the incredible beauty and splendor of nature, feeling that my life was just a speck of dust in the vast universe. Then I had an idea, why am I here? If I thought something important It doesn't really matter, so what's important? What's the point of my existence? Why am I here?"

"After those questions popped up, I was just as Kayleen told you. Until I figured it out. Answer, the problem disappears."

I was leaning back in my chair, but when Jacob was talking, I unconsciously leaned towards him, trying to hear every part of what he said.

"Thank you, Jacob. The story is amazing."

"John, life is amazing. It's just that there are people who don't realize they're authors and that they can write what they want."

Jacob stood up and said, "I'm going back to the kitchen . Clean up. John, do you want anything else to eat?"

"No, I'm leaving soon. I was completely lost before I found

this place. Now, I still don't know where I should go."

Jacob smiled and said, "It depends on where you want to go."

He opened his mouth to say something else, and paused again, as if he was determined not to say it. He turned to something else: "You drive a few miles down this road and you'll see an intersection. Turn right and you'll be back on the freeway. There's a gas station near the entrance to the freeway. You've got enough gas left to get your car there."

I don't know how he knew I had enough gas left to get me to the gas station, but I had a gut feeling that he was right. I stood up and held out my hand: "Thank you, Jacob, your café is so special."

He shook my hand. "No thanks, John. Good luck." He turned and walked away.

20

I looked down at the menu.

Why are you here?

Are you afraid of death?

Are you satisfied?

These questions are profound. If someone had asked me this a day ago, I would have thought he was a little unhinged. Now, sitting here, looking at the back of the menu, I can't imagine myself before.

Kayleen came to the table, put my bill on the table, and handed me a lunch box: "This is the last piece of strawberry rhubarb pie, Jacob's farewell gift to you."

"This is my gift to you. ." She said and handed me a menu. On the cover of the menu, under "Why did you come to this cafe", Kayleen wrote me a sentence. I read it twice.

"A little thing to keep you as a souvenir." She said with a smile.

"Thank you, Kayleen. Thank you for everything you've done for me."

"I'm honored, John. It's our fate."

I put the money on the table, grabbed the menu and the pie box, and walked out of the cafe , into the beginning of a new day.

The sun is about to rise behind the woods across from the parking lot, and a new day is coming. There was still a trace of silence from last night in the air, but the hustle and bustle of the day had already begun.

Feeling energized and reinvigorated, I switched the lunch box from my right to my left and opened the door.

"Why am I here?" I thought, "Why am I here..."

It was a brand new day indeed.

21

After a night at that cafe, my life changed. These changes didn't come as quickly and suddenly as a flash of lightning, but they had the same power and ultimately had an impact on my life.

Like Beth, I also started to slowly change. I can't stop thinking "why am I here" when I leave the cafe, and then I can't stop thinking about it for the rest of my vacation. I didn't get an answer right away. I knew it wasn't enough to just take a vacation to think about it, and then go back to the life I used to be, to find out what my existence—or PFE, as Kayleen called it—was. As with most insights, the answer to this question takes some thought to find.

I learned various methods from Kayleen and Beth, and finally, I combined these methods and finally came up with the answer. In the beginning, I set aside a small time each day to focus on what I enjoyed doing, much like Beth did. Then I started trying to find and take advantage of those opportunities Kayleen said, to get in touch and learn about new things. As a result, the answer to the question, "Why am I here?" becomes wider and less narrow than it was at the beginning of my trip.

Finally, my PFE and the way I want to implement it became clear. Ironically, I figured it out in the face of the most difficult challenges. When there are two choices in front of you: one is to pursue your own meaning in life, and the other is to live, you may think that making this decision is easy.

but it is not the truth.

Over time, I've found that most people's journeys end here. They peek into the little holes in the fence and see clearly the kind of life they want to live, but for some reason they won't open the door and walk into that life.

At first, this fact made me feel particularly sorry. But as Jacob said, I've come to believe that different people make choices at different stages of life, some people make choices as children, some people grow up, and some people don't make choices in their lives. There is no rush to make a choice, no one can help you choose, you can only make it yourself.

"If you've done what you want to do, or are doing what you want to do every day, there's no reason to be afraid of losing the opportunity to do those things." For me, that's what helped me push that aside. door. Today, this sentence has become my life's creed.

I often think of that cafe. Every time I open my letterbox and see it stuffed with ads and messages I don't need, I'm reminded of Kayleen and her green turtle. The reverse wave never stopped, waiting for an opportunity to take away my time and energy. But now that I know it exists, I can preserve my strength and ride the positive waves.

I also often think about Jacob's story on the beach in Costa Rica. From a macro perspective, our stress, anxiety, victories and defeats are all insignificant.

However, it is precisely because we face our seemingly insignificant selves that we find the meaning of life.

If I have any regrets about changing my life, it's that I really regret not making it sooner. I thought I might not be ready until that night at the cafe.

Now, I understand the meaning of my existence, and I will work hard to achieve this meaning. On the other side of the door, I'll never go back.

www.ingramcontent.com/pod-product-compliance
Lightning Source LLC
Chambersburg PA
CBHW031451150726
47990CB00007B/2704